BEHIND THE WAI

Behind the Wall
& Other Stories

TOM KELLY

Postbox
PRESS

First published in 2018 by Postbox Press,
the literary fiction imprint of Red Squirrel Press
36 Elphinstone Crescent
Biggar
South Lanarkshire
ML12 6GU
www.redsquirelpress.com

Typeset and designed by Gerry Cambridge
in Baskerville 10 Pro and 120 Pro
gerry.cambridge@btinternet.com

Image of bricks on front cover: d13/Shutterstock.com

A CIP catalogue record for this book is available from
the British Library.

ISBN: 978 1 910437 46 9

Red Squirrel Press is committed to a sustainable future.
This book is printed in the UK by Imprint Digital using
Forest Stewardship Council certified paper.

FSC
www.fsc.org
MIX
Paper from
responsible sources
FSC® C004309

Contents

THE BOYS ARE PELTING EGGS at his window. Joe throws the telephone down, his daughter telling him to be careful with his bad heart. She hates these Sunday afternoon telephone calls as it's always fraught before and after them. She tells him to take it easy but he never listens. He could live with her. He wouldn't. Wouldn't leave his home, his town, 'I'll die here.' His usual response.

Joe's at war. He storms out of the back door, tells the boys to stop it. That they are scum. Forgets his prepared speech. The boys give him v signs, mocking Joe and Churchill and anybody else for that matter. The boys hunt in packs. Terrorise the estate. Their woollen hats pulled down almost over their eyes, creating double worried frowns. They don't hate Joe but can't understand why he goes on and on. They start dancing in front of him. Take Bruce Lee stances.

They chant, 'Joe, Joe, Joe.'

Kicking their heavy boots toward him. The biggest, the one with the most tattoos, that took drugs first, hates best, kicks Joe in the face. Joe bleeds and kicks back. They rush and hit him. They want him to stop hassling them and let him know they have some power. He has to see that. And got to know it's the only thing they have. Joe's veins stand to attention. His head buzzes. He falls on the path in the back garden, grazes his knees, bangs his head and as the swelling on his head grows, dies. The boys scatter like a crowd in front of a tidal wave. From above, the patterns are akin to images in a kaleidoscope: the white path, boys' black hats, running off into star-studded patterns and to the right there is Joe. Dead.

See them run across fields. A pack of six, the nearest they have ever been to a family. Running through the estate, kicking over dustbins, chasing dogs into swirling fights. Breath comes in gasps. They are birds in a storm, struggling over their battered landscape. Grunting. Pushing into each other as if they had no place to live. Running above earth that's made shit of them. They hope they are heading towards some sort of salvation. Being saved, without giving into the evangelical brigade and having to clap your hands for Jesus. And still they run. Not towards a beautiful sunset. It's too late for that. Not to some saviour. They feel this in their bones as their boots grind the earth and their gimlet eyes hit another estate where nothing shocks or saves, just lives on the edge of nothing.

They know the police, doctor and priest have been to Joe's and they will have to stop running but it's always been like this. Being chased by mothers, fathers and boyfriends that hate for kicks, carrying this knowledge like broken nails lodged in their stomachs. Scrabbling into a block of flats they know which ones are empty and bad news travels quickly: Joe is dead. The boys are shocked. Drugs

and thieving they know, breathing them in like nec-
tar in their dark lives. Yet death is something new
to them and they know someone must be blamed.
They examine each other; share guilt as if doling
out cigarettes. They killed Joe as good as sticking
a knife in him. Made a good job of it. Dead before
he hit the ground. Killed him like a sniper. Like in
video games. Like everywhere but in real life. Joe
told them that they would kill him.

One of the boys knocks off a load of lager. They
drink believing there will never be a tomorrow
and they know there won't be for Joe. They feel
as if they are trapped in a huge fridge on a summer's day. Joe is somehow here and is marching
among them. Knocking cans out of their hands,
saying they are too young. Telling them to stand
up straight and don't slouch. Joe was a pain. Joe
caused them bother. Nowt but trouble. Icy sobs rise
out of their chests. Warm tears and lager rising up,
as they shout, 'More. More. More.'

They chant and chant as lager disappears down
angry throats. They dance to music played so loud
it hurts. Next door batter their door as the boys
open windows and give the world their screams.
The world that's done this to them. They don't say.

Joe was a laugh. They loved him. Shock and alcohol combining as they cry self-pity tears. Joe's
daughter is sobbing as the boys fling empty cans
out of the windows. Next morning light catches
them asleep, six pups spread among the debris of a
stranger's once-home. In all their dreams they have

been chased by Joe and Bruce Lee who turned on them. He kicked them over rooftops; the pain was real, not like in the films. The blows burst blood vessels. They spat blood and pleaded with Bruce to stop. Some sit hunched against walls. Music branded to their ears. The volume hurts but they need this pain. They try to cut out everything as they mumble the words to the songs. Others lie on their backs, pick out faces in the ceiling, joining the dots and there is only one face that emerges. Time is glued.

The boys wake, remembrance twitching in their leaden eyes. They scrabble among battered cartons for something that is not dead: a lick of milk or lager, a bite of bread and there is still Joe. The police shudder at the door. The boys know what will happen. It has been passed down from tenement blocks, bedsits to sofa surfing.

'All houses, never homes.' The social worker would tell Joe. Everyone knows this but rotten eggs struggling down his windows and broken fences and flowers trampled and red roses painted black and acid on the lawn and darts in the door and all this Joe suffered. All of this accurate list the boys inflicted. Now the boys are being interviewed and they follow instructions and say nowt to no-one. The boys know the police and how they stand with them, what to expect and that they will get nothing. Others promise better lives; homes without debt, with no crime, where children are cared for and even loved.

The police say, 'Sit there.'

They separate them and ask if they want a solicitor and their 'guardians.' They never say, 'mother,' or 'father,' using the correct terminology, knowing full well the boys' 'circumstances.' That is another word they use. Their histories transparent, faces displaying every intimate detail. The police ask questions and the boys mumble as silence rings like a drill in each of their heads.

Joe's daughter breathes guilt; he could have lived with her. He was too independent. She should have insisted and he would be here, telling her not to worry. Her shocking cries are violent and guilt's a great stone in her head. Joe's friends dig out black ties and memories for his funeral. The daughter blames herself again and again, and the boys' families everyone but themselves. Dark clouds gather. The boys cry in cells. They slouch against walls and Joe's daughter cannot forgive them.

'Joe's dead.'

And blame must be left on someone's unwelcome mat.

• *The New Tracksuit* •

BREATHING'S HARSH. LUNGS BURN. Grass, at the side of the track, inviting. He is turning white with the effort of this training session. Arms swing across his chest as he clings to the bend of the running track's swaying washed-out white lines. This is the last run of the night. 'Maintain the pace,' he says to himself, crossing the spot where his tracksuit lies. Every run is in the same time. His head hangs between shaking legs as he gulps air, drags off his vest, struggles into the tracksuit, tripping every time he tries to put his feet into the bottoms. He jogs haltingly home, drained.

The next day, at work, his calf muscles are stiff; he had given himself a hard work-out and that it is what he wanted. It had to hurt. 'Pain leads to victory,' is one of his mantras. Now the best middle-distance runner in the athletics club: he did not want to be an also-ran. Hated that idea. Pain proved he would make it. He trained alone. No-one in the club was as serious as Mickey.

They would say, 'Steer clear of Mickey.'

Then, under their breath, 'He'll kill himself.'

'Alright son?'

Mickey's father was used to long pauses. Today was no exception.

'I could come to the track with you and hold the stop watch?'

Mickey looked at him, his thoughts miles away, wanting no-one to find out how well training was going. He is so much faster than last year and it was still only May. He was frightened to say.

'I'd rather be by myself,' is his eventual response.

His father had been met by, 'thanks but no thanks,' since his mother's death. Mickey had always been quiet but now rarely spoke unless prompted out of his silence. It was unnerving. His father offered to buy him training gear. His tracksuit looked past its best but Mickey didn't seem to notice. He did not want anyone to get close to him. Wanted nothing from his father. From no-one.

He had his races planned: the county championships, 'The Northern' and then the 'Nationals' in July. He was hoping for an international vest this year but told no-one because he did not want to see their looks of scorn, or worse pity.

The next night he warmed-up for half an hour until he was sweating. He did not want to train: did not want the hurt. He was not a masochist but pain eventually brought glory. He fed on glory. When he cried in his bedroom it was for himself. No one would get near him. His success was not going to be shared with some athletic guru; it would be down to him: Mickey Mills. He began training and had to hold himself back as he was running so fast. He was smiling. A great broad smile. The wind hollowed his face, made tears spring in his eyes. 'I'm flying,' he said over and over.

The following Saturday, at the county championship, he warmed-up very slowly and had an easy heat. He knew all the lads running against him. Some joked as they jogged to the start line. Mickey was silent. What he needed to do was finish in the first three but not push too hard. Make it as easy as possible. There was a scramble to the first bend; he nearly fell onto the track. He hung at the back of the pack. The first lap was far too fast and the rest were suffering. The pace dropped dramatically on the second lap and that suited him. He was ambling and nonchalantly went into the lead in a near-trance.

It was the announcer, with, 'It's number seven, Mills in the lead,' that woke him and he slowed the pace. The third lap was easy; it was only at the bell he felt any real exertion and on the back straight he opened up a gap and finally crossed the line in front. Putting on his tracksuit and watching the next heat he knew he could win his first county championship. He did. Strangers patted him on the back. He got the bus home alone and had an early night. The local paper ran a paragraph telling of his victory. People noticed. The boss at work spoke to him for the first time. His dad asked him to go for a pint. He said no. He had an early night with the words of the article ringing in his head, 'Mills Wins.' He wanted more but knew he had to concentrate, not get carried away.

The next night at the athletics club he was greeted by a mix of concealed envy and congratulations.

The Club Secretary shook his hand. Mickey smiled and walked away. He was going it alone and did not need their help. Where had they been this past year? No-one had spoken, shaken his hand and patted his back during the long winter months. Two or three watched him training. He soon forgot them. Three weeks to the day was the Northern Championships and each session was planned. Life had to be like that if you wanted success. He had to blot everything out, except what he needed. He was vaguely aware of his dad wanting to help.

Collecting his race number, he checked to see who had reported for the race. The favourites were there. The Northern Championships were an important step. His heat was at two. The final, the last race of the day, at five. Not for the first time he felt like a monk. Some of the runners were talkative. He preferred silence. They laughed in a forced manner. The first three in each heat and the two fastest losers got through to the final. He wanted to run within himself but ran a terrible race, running too fast and then too slowly and finished third after a sprint finish. He was exhausted. There was a metallic taste in his mouth and his chest was sore. He hoped he would recover in time for the final. He went back to the changing rooms and had to be alone. There was someone sitting beside his running gear.

This stranger began to talk, 'Mickey Mills, isn't it?'

Mickey was going to give him the silent treatment,

or tell him to clear off but did not want to risk getting himself upset before the final. He grunted a reply.

'You can still win.' The stranger continued.

Mickey softened. Part of him wanted to listen. He was at a low ebb and this man was not caught up in him winning. He was talking when they both knew he had run badly.

'Who the hell was he?' Thought Mickey, taking off his race vest. The stranger did not take the hint and go away.

I said, 'you can still win.'

He went on, 'You've got to dominate the race. Get in front. Run the race at an even pace. Not the way you ran, you have taken a lot out of yourself. You're going to have to out psych them. Wear this.'

He pointed at Mickey's battered gear.

'That's alright for Tough of the Track but it cuts no ice here. You have got to look the part.' He threw over a bag with what Mickey thought was a garish tracksuit. 'Who was he?'

'I run a sports shop and used to run myself.'

Answering Mickey's unasked question. Mickey's chest pain had subsided. The metallic taste had gone.

'Wear the gear, look like a winner and you're half-way there.'

The conversation was making him forget the hurt of his bad run and looking at his new tracksuit, lying like priests' vestments by his side: he was letting someone into his life. Mentally pushing away the tracksuit, he turned around to say, 'No thanks,' but the intruder had gone.

Some of the other finalists began to get changed in the adjacent room. They were talking as if Mickey were a country hick, laughing about him. He could not believe it. Had the sports shop man set the whole thing up? He was in a rage with tightness across his chest and was on the brink of tears. When the other athletes were gone he found a quiet corner to doze for an hour.

Before the final he took off the old tracksuit and pushed it into his bag. He pulled out the new one and an envelope fell to the floor. He recognized his dad's hand writing. Putting on the new tracksuit he felt he had grown six inches. He had recovered and was the first to the starting line, striding away from the rest of the field, then running back to them on his toes.

At the gun he sprung into the lead. The first lap was at a steady pace, he was breathing hard but it was controlled. At the half way point he was suffering but showing nothing. One of the favourite's moved onto Mickey's shoulder, testing him. He picked up the pace. They met the bell neck and neck. He pushed away from Mickey and for the first time he was second but did not panic. Mickey came onto his shoulder and kicked and kicked. He had the lead. The finish seemed to be moving further away as he heard harsh breathing. He was being attacked, his legs were dead. He was running underwater as he threw himself at the line with his legs aping Bambi. People smiled and guided him to his tracksuit. He had won and his lips trembled.

At the presentation, he stood like an embarrassed school boy. While he waited, he pulled his dad's envelope from his bag. He read the first few lines without really taking in too much in and then his dad's voice began to register.

'I knew you wouldn't take the tracksuit from me so I asked the manager of the sports shop to give it to you, he said he had been a runner himself and that he was going to the championships and would give it to you. Whatever happens Mickey, I am proud of you son.'

It was then Mickey gave into tears.

• *The Dream* •

A GREYING BACON RIND OF canvas curls by their bedroom door, a thin rug is almost lost beside the bed where the old couple lie back-to-back. The old man dreams. He sees himself in the shipyard where he worked most of his life, throwing ropes high as the sky. Looking at the bird-like dock-side cranes, their arms hanging in mourning, he begins to work as a rigger, a skill learnt on the training ship at twelve. Holding a rope in his soft palms he deftly makes a knot, throws it and is surprised at how long it takes to land; it seems to stand in mid-air before coiling round the ship's deck rail. As far as he can see there is nothing to be done, he was getting paid for doing nowt.

He gives a gummy smile and says, 'Mar-vill-us.'

His voice echoes across the river and sings further up the Tyne. He sits on a low wall eyeing boat upon boat snuggling together, and realises there will be a fair bit of docking in the next few days. He smokes his pipe, spits into the dock bottom, pulls tobacco shag from his brown leather pouch and fills his pipe, patting down the tobacco, before slowly lighting and sucking its grey stem. Finally, he lets out smoke that breezes from his bulbous lips.

He thinks of the past: he has time to do that. He was placed in the boys' home at ten-year-old, the register's bald statement said.

'With What Charge: Non Compliance.'

Hiding a simple truth: he was illegitimate and his mother could not work and look after him. His mother said his father was a sailor. She said little else. He didn't ask. He wishes he had.

Outside the couple's bedroom it is still dark and frost grips the path to their door. His wife wakes a number of times before eventually settling into sleep. She sees herself in Ireland, even though she has never been. She wants to be there in this dream. It is warm, frost is forgotten and she can hear a plaintive lament being played in the distance.

'This is Ireland,' she whispers as if not wanting anyone to know. Her father left Galway to work in the Tyneside shipyards. She pictures him walking home from work and her mother appears, linking her father's arm. They have a baby and she smiles as her parents disappear. She prays she will see them later.

The old man's face looks troubled. He is dreaming of his war. He is on a truck and has dysentery and does not want to be reminded of that. He needs a dream with comfort, not that horror. In their bedroom, ice has formed and died on the inside of the window. Outside it is becoming light; footprints stamped on the frost are retreating like war in the old man's dream. He is with his wife by the seaside, they are young, and it is summer. This is the sort of dream he wants. The sky is a sparkly bright blue as they ride on the top deck of a tram. He looks smart; you could cut yourself on the creases in his trousers.

His wife wears a hat with a feather that waves as they walk to the pier head. He has never seen her look so attractive. He will tell her. Not one cloud annoys the sun. He dreams on and he is beside a boat and sees a young couple going aboard; they smile at him and wave as if cleaning a huge invisible window. They mouth, 'Come on, come on.'

He realises, for the first time in years, he is happy. He taps the tobacco out of his pipe onto the shipyard floor and places it in the top pocket of his jacket. He checks the sky and it is still clear and decides to follow the young couple that look like him and his wife when they were young. The old man is smiling in his dream.

His wife approaches him in her dream. She can see he is happy as she begins to wake and be aware of their bedroom: the crucifix on the wall and below the dressing table which houses her husband's war medals in an oval, gold case. She knows every inch of this room, behind the door is a dark painted hook where her dressing gown hangs. It looks as if someone is clinging to the door, onto life itself. She is an old woman and will die in a year or two at home; on her terms, not surrounded by strangers. No-one will touch upon her moment of death.

As she rises and shuffles across the cold canvas, bed clothes follow like a warm wave. Wrapping herself in a dressing gown, the bed's warmth still on her, she edges towards the door, her slippers shushing over the uneven floor. It is eight o'clock and her dream is facing the morning. She glances toward her husband but his face is hidden by bedclothes.

Going downstairs, wishing the stairs were not so steep, she shudders from stair to stair. The embers of the coal fire still glow; her husband always banks up the fire before they go to bed. A wisp of smoke curls up the chimney and with the poker she lances the fire, revealing its red heart below. The Sacred Heart, for her, is alive in the fire and on the wall where a huge print dominates; its bleeding heart she too often felt was hers. Drinking a cup of tea, she offers up a prayer for her family and herself. She knows there will be more pain and sorrow but believes in the power of prayer, it gives her a strength lacking in her body. She tries to recall her dream; it is something to cling to.

She knows what to do. Next door have a telephone; they will ring the doctor and the priest. She pulls the bed clothes around him and recalls the dream and sits beside her husband and prays as her wedding ring slips on her thin finger. She leaves the bedroom curtains drawn and holds onto the dream.

• *Elsie* •

I'VE JUST LOST ONE BOYFRIEND, Tommy. He was going to ask to marry me. I thought, 'Get in there, while he's still got a pulse.' In the time we were courting he never called me Elsie, it was always his wife's name, Teresa. I got used to it. He had dementia. We would walk and talk about years ago, in the end I thought I had been to that caravan at Seahouses. And I felt I had the four bairns to him. They hardly ever visited; I asked one of them and she said she found it 'upsetting.' Her own father. I'm glad I never had her as a daughter.

Some women would say, 'Why should I have an old man to look after?'

I wouldn't have the 'bother,' they'd look after him in the residential home. I never married and it's one of my ambitions before I go. I don't just mean *go* from here to another residential home but to the crematorium; you know, twenty minutes in and out and back here for sausage rolls and weak tea. It's not a lot to ask. I want it to say 'Mrs.' on my death certificate.

Somebody's been smoking in here. Hanging is too good for them. They try to smoke in our little garden but I have this 'Stop Smoking' sign and a big pair of pliers. I stare at the smokers and point to the sign. They swear under their breath, then stub out the cigarette. I use my cigarette obliterator, which collects the filthy thing and burn it in my mini-incinerator.

As I was saying, it's funny saying, 'boyfriend,' when Tommy was nearly ninety. He had worked as a shipwright on the Tyne. I must have built a dozen ships with him walking round that garden. He could remember every detail of each ship but didn't know what day it was. I'm eighty-seven. I know I'm in good nick. You can see that. I've always looked after meself. Never smoked or drank. There's no need for it. My first boyfriend, when I was eighteen, said, he wanted to smoke a pipe, it was fashionable. I said it's either the pipe or me. I never missed him.

The thing I like about this place is that they keep changing the staff. In the five years, three months I've been here there have been seventeen women looking after our floor. Everyone's been a right floozy. Talking to the men and giggling with them. I've seen things that would turn your hair grey, if it wasn't already. Billy wanted only me in the end. Mind I had to, 'go deaf,' when he asked for a cigarette. I used to talk about my past with Tommy because I knew he would forget what I'd said. I would tell him everything and ten minutes later he couldn't remember a thing. I liked that, nobody knowing anything about me.

I worked down Birmingham. This lad was always chasing after me. Big he was. Big nose, eyes, ears. When he was right up close it was like having a magnifying glass in front of your eyes. He kissed me once. Once was enough. He proposed. God, the thought of having children with elephant faces: I wouldn't have been able to sleep at night. He drank. He said he didn't but at Christmas I smelt drink on his breath. He said he had just had the one sherry. That was it. What else could I do? I can't even remember his name but for years I used to dream of waking up with an elephant lying beside me.

Tommy never drank in here but I had to work hard at stopping him. One of the floozies used to give him cigarettes. I reported her. She called me every name under the sun. I saw her husband; he used to pick her up: beer belly and nicotine fingers. A real treasure. The day of Tommy's funeral all his family turned-up: hypocrites. I had never seen them for months and there they were, smoking and drinking and telling stories about when he used to go to the club and how it was sad he never got out, then looking at me. As if I was a leper. I could have told them a few home truths but I decided against it. I didn't go to the cemetery, he was getting buried with Teresa, it would have been like burying meself. She never drank or smoked. I would have liked her. She must have been a very good woman. Tommy's family came back to the home after the funeral and said I had made his last months hell. Stopping him from smoking and having the odd pint at the club. That was his only enjoyment, they said. They presented me with a box of Havana cigars and a bottle of whiskey. I would not have them in my room; I sold them to the staff.

After Birmingham and 'Elephant Face,' I moved

to London. It was one big ashtray. I went in a bar, just the once, with this man from work, he drank like a fish and smoked like a chimney. I thought I could change him. Let me tell you, it never works: once a smoker, always a smoker. He was on his Stag night, the day before our wedding, and I caught him in a pub smoking and drinking. I watched through the pub's smoky windows and he was laughing and you mightn't believe this, but he had three cigarettes in his mouth at one time. I marched into the bar, handed back the engagement ring, went to my lodgings and packed: The best day's work I have ever done.

After London I came back home but I didn't live with my family, they had moved and I didn't have their address. We had lost contact over the years. I think Christmas cards are such a waste. I worked in the Civil Service. I had my own section; it was the most efficient in the place. They were all girls and none were married. I discouraged it. I had them in the office and explained the pitfalls of marriage and said that they would not get a reference from me. They did not smoke or drink. Every morning I would check their fingernails for any sign of nicotine. I liked to stamp it out before it got a hold.

They've got a new man coming in; his family came round and said they liked the place. They stood outside, near the door, talking for ages and one of them cried. He is a chronic asthmatic. When they're like that they are easier to control. Stop them smoking and drinking. Then you've got a chance with them, that's my philosophy. If you meet the new residents on the first day here, it makes a big impression: a smiling face, a caring voice. I always say, 'I hope you enjoy your stay here. I'd like to be your friend.'

Then I smile and open my arms. It works every time. The Manager always says, 'Here's the welcoming committee.'

The staff appreciates what I do. I can tell.

This new man's been good-looking in his time. They say he was married twice, I'm not surprised. Mind, he can really move with that Zimmer, like a greyhound out of a trap. I'll catch him. I always do. This is his room. Very tidy. I like to see that in a man. John's his name. No sign of cigarettes. Trousers neatly folded, shoes polished. I think a man's wardrobe says a lot about him. I am impressed. He's in bed. That's fortunate. I have tried to speak to him since he arrived; he must be a bit deaf, but, as I said, I catch them in the end, I always do.

'Hello. H...e...l...l...o. What? You can't breathe. I'm the same. That's what old age is about: loss of breath, dignity, bowel control and incontinence. You've got to get used to it.'

He seems to be smiling; I don't think he's short of breath. I can tell he wants to kiss me. I don't mind. I don't blame him.

'Yes, I'll give you a kiss. Is that nice? I thought it would be.'

He is going blue. I must be standing on his oxygen line. I will put on my wedding veil. I thought it might come in handy.

His eyes seem to be saying, 'Will you marry me?'

I can tell. I'll not shout for the nurse. There's just him and me.

'Do you take this woman for your lawful wedded wife?'

Just nod. That's right.

'Yes, I take this man as my lawful wedded husband. I do. I do.'

• *The Running Boy* •

H E SITS AT THE BACK OF THE CLASS. The teach-er's blurred voice miles away as if speaking in a distant swimming baths. Teachers suspect drugs. Everyone leaves a force-field around him fearing his touch will shrivel them. He attends school most days but is never really there. His fingernails are filled with dirt and uniform hangs by a thread. His brown eyes and black hair suggest a Mediterranean background he has never considered. At one time he created interest and pity but now he is too far away, everyone agrees. In the Staff Room there is a grumbling agreement: he is a lost cause.

The boy leaves school alone. His jacket ham-mocks from him as his belly ruptures over his too tight trousers. Shoes and socks reveal gaping holes. No one tags along beside him. School is forgotten as he trundles to a shop. He buys crisps and can of lemonade. Coins rattle in his top pocket. He is served with a mannered indifference. The shop-keeper does not like this fat boy.

He is shocked when his mother shouts, 'James,' and doesn't think it can be him. He is genuinely surprised someone knows his name. His mother has not seen him in weeks. She is fixated with her new boyfriend who stands in shadow outside the bar, his cigarette weaving from his long fingers. She holds her son for a moment and places cash in his top pocket, knowing where he keeps his money. The one thing she does know about him as she asks him to smile for her boyfriend. He forms a smile as if slowly making concrete. The man walks toward him and takes his mother's hand, and without speaking they topple off together. Her heels clack on the pavement as the boy walks home eating crisps that stick to his full lips. Soon he cannot picture his mother.

He does not have a front door key. He clambers over the back wall. The old man sits by the fire and raises his head as the boy enters. They don't speak. The old man's head is lost to the fire that crackles with the wood he places carefully on top of the cinders. They both appear golden as flames rise. The old man should not be here but he has nowhere else to go. He came dragging a heavy suit case and the boy pointed to what was going to be his mother's bedroom. Now they play with silence. It is an instrument they love, creating noises: the scraping of the old man's shoes across the bare floor, the smacking of the old man's hands when the fire begins to glow. They sit. Old man and boy. Happy with silence. The old man has slipped off everyone's register. His family have forgotten him. One son moved away. Wife dead. Daughter lost to him. She died young. He does not want to think about that.

Night cuts in. The boy wears a battered tracksuit. One of his mother's boyfriends gave it to him. He can't recall his name or face.

'One of the many,' more than one have said.

He doesn't want to think about that. The old man

goes to bed, turns and looks at the boy in the track-suit and nods his head. The boy notices this. They know one another's every movement. Silence they have learnt to live with, and looks and movement have become a new vocabulary, like the stars: distant but understandable.

On the boy's birthday the mother turned up. She kept the taxi running as she gave him a card and present she did not have time to wrap. At the banging on the front door the old man headed to the bedroom. His mother looks at nothing. She gives him money from her bulging bag. When the new boyfriend comes into the room their drink dressed breath pollutes the air. They begin to sing, 'Happy Birthday,' until they remember the taxi and run off without saying goodbye, without ending the song. The old man looks out of the broken window at the boy's mother falling into the taxi and spits into the fire and decides to speak later.

The boy stopped going to school. The address in the school's records was four or five rented flats ago. His mother's mobile was seven ago. Authorities decided they had left the area. A rubber stamp made that claim. The old man and boy began a new regime. There had never been order in the boy's life. He took every day as it came. His father, he recalled, was tall and dark but that might have been another of his mother's boyfriends.

'He left years ago,' is all his mother ever said.

She drank. Flirted. Had late nights. They moved from rented flat to rented flat. He imagined this was everyone's routine. He went to six or seven schools. Liked none better or worse than any other.

They got up early. Bought food. Not just crisps, bread and lemonade. The old man showed the boy how to cook. They would begin by washing their hands. The old man pointed to the boys fingernails and said they should be clean. This was almost new to the boy, like a distant memory. They began to tidy the house. Bought a brush and shovel and cleared the dog and cat shit from the back yard. Filled the dustbin with the dirt that had gathered in the flat. The boy began to notice change. The old man became cleaner and so did the boy.

Nights were for stories. The old man and boy sat either side of the fire. The old man had not really spoken for years. He knew he had to do one thing: let the boy see. Show him there was more than the litany of failure he had endured. A sense of duty was something the old man was recalling. Running was something the old man remembered and there was no pain surrounding those memories. The old man began his stories.

'I began to run and get away from everything I didn't like or understand.'

A father that hit him before speaking. A mother who wanted to be young forever. The stories of running began every night. The boy drank in each word.

They had been to the library and joined for the first time and read about the great Australian runner

Herb Elliott and his coach Percy Cerutty. The boy began to run in his dreams. He told the old man who said that is how it begins but when you run in the real world, you must not stop. You have a duty to yourself and to running. Work hard every day. The boy did not answer: he did not understand. One morning, as he and the old man walked to the Green Market, where they bought all their vegetables, he caught his reflection in a shop window: he was a thin boy with an old man.

His mother banged on the door. Screamed into their front room. Her boyfriend had beaten her and said he no longer loved her. She smelt of dried perspiration and stale drink. She threw herself on the floor. When her mobile rang the boy answered. It was her boyfriend. He was in a taxi on his way to pick her up. He told his mother and she ran to the toilet and re-appeared minutes later smiling and handed the boy a fistful of money, 'For crisps and stuff.'

She ran out of the door as the taxi reversed and never said goodbye. The old man took the money and laid it on the table. It remained there all night. The next day the boy said he had to go somewhere. The old man nodded his worried head. The money was gone as he carried-out their daily routine alone and headed to the Green Market and the butchers. He began preparing their meal. The boy returned and placed parcels on the table. They ate their meal before the boy smiled and produced a pair of running shoes, tracksuit and vest. For the first time in his life something had begun.

• *Behind the Wall* •

B RIDGET AND TOMMY LIVE comfortably. They
have been careful. Tommy has never been a
drinker; the odd sherry at Christmas is his limit.
Bridget, as a child in the 1930s, had seen the results
of too much drink.

'Drink's for fools,' she would say. Bridget is no
fool.

They are settled in their retirement. Tommy was
a labourer in the Tyne shipyards. On Friday nights
he would always come home to Bridget with an un-
opened wage packet. Not for him hiding how much
he earned from his wife.

It's 1963. They have just moved into their new
council house on an estate that had been fields only
a few short years before. The first week in the house
Tommy would switch the electric light off and on as
Bridget told him to, 'Act your age.'

They were new-fangled and he loved this house
smelling of fresh paint, with the luxury of an inside
toilet and 'partial central heating.' Everything has a
place as their mantelpiece bears witness; it's a mini
forest of knick-knacks. The sitting room is warm
and the coal fire banked-up, with no ash in the
hearth: everything is in order. Passers-by, at night,
might catch Tommy reading, usually a Western,
while Bridget knits and sews. Both with a rapt look
of attention.

'I see they're knocking down High Street.' Tommy reads from the newspaper. Adding, with a smile, 'Happy days.'

Bridget's reply is terse, 'We were eaten alive by bugs.'

'That was our first house.' Tommy, as usual, tries to recall better memories. Their remembrances begin, story after story running into each other. Bridget recalls the McCanns and their Saturday night fights, 'The drink's got a lot to answer for.'

The fire glows but its comfort's forgotten. Tommy thinks of the McCanns' daughter and says to Bridget, 'You brought up that lass.'

It is some time before Bridget replies, 'TB was a killer. I could have cried and never stopped.'

Tommy breaks in with, 'That we couldn't have any children of our own?'

She does not reply and the air rings with a silence you can taste. He stands, draws the curtains, winds up the clock; the habits of a life-time he carries like a scar. They climb the stairs to bed, memories hanging on every step.

Unusually Tommy gets up late after a restless night, makes two cups of tea and returns to their bedroom where Bridget is preoccupied. She saw grey washing lines of smoke hanging from the coal fire last night and knew there would be a visitor. Tommy is making the fire and the hearth's piled with cinders. He wipes his face and leaves a cross of dust over his cheeks. The young policeman rattles on the door. Tommy invites him into the house and Bridget is shocked as he walks into their living room. Here is the stranger Bridget feared. She doesn't have a chance to comb her hair. To make matters worse Tommy's face is covered in dust. What will the policeman think? She can't concentrate on what he's saying although she's looking at him intently. It is certain phrases that register and she finds herself repeating in her head what he is saying.

'I have some rather disturbing news. I believe you lived at 23 High Street?'

Tommy dived in too quickly for Bridget's liking, with, 'They're knocking it down.'

The policeman, fearing Tommy would regale him with stories of the house years ago, carries on with,

'There is no easy way to say this but the skeleton of a child has been found behind the wall of the house you once occupied.'

Bridget's scream is followed by the policeman offering to make a pot of tea. They decline. Tommy and Bridget sit encased in the past. The policeman apologises, 'I am really sorry. I can see it's been a terrible shock.'

Neither Bridget nor Tommy take him to the door. They do not move as the fire stays dead. Bridget is the first to speak, in barely a whisper,

'We used to pray for a baby in that house, kneeling side-by-side. I closed my eyes and believed our prayers would be answered.'

Her voice doesn't so much as stop but slowly trail away. Tommy looks at Bridget and sees how close she is to tears as he places an arm around her. He eventually speaks, 'We would have looked after the bairn.'

They give into tears that have waited until they could wait no more. Seeing Bridget crying is rare and Tommy is at a loss how to cope, clinging to her, fearing she will crumble. They sit as the fire remains unlit and the coal dust on Tommy's face becomes a stigmata for a long-dead child. In a worrying silence, they eventually clean the house and light the fire as Bridget wishes the policeman could come now. Fancy seeing them like that.

'Whose baby was it?'

Tommy's one thought he holds dead in his head. He wants to ask Bridget how she feels but she speaks first, 'Cat got your tongue?'

'I was thinking, that's all,' Tommy says.

'I wondered what the noise was,' Bridget quips.

She remains distant. He is silent. Time trundles on, sun filters through the curtains as a sparrow ferrets on their bird table. Normally they would have watched its antics but today it's ignored. Tommy can't stand the silence any longer, 'You know who lived upstairs?'

Bridget's reply is brevity itself, 'The McCanns.'

Mrs McCann had a daughter before she married McCann. Both Bridget and Tommy could never bring themselves to say McCann's Christian name. That might have softened their feelings towards him. He was a drunken, jealous man who hated the sight of his step-daughter Margaret. She would say she was going on her 'holidays' downstairs, staying for days with Bridget and Tommy. Bridget thought of McCann and felt physically sick.

Tommy says, 'It's in tonight's paper.'

He begins to read, 'Forensic experts are investigating the discovery of a skeleton found in the town today.'

Tommy's face hardens, 'McCann died four or five years ago. I heard the family didn't go to the funeral.'

'That doesn't surprise me,' says Bridget.

Bridget's love for Margaret is resurrected as Tommy makes the umpteenth cup of tea and, for the first time in what seems an eternity, Bridget looks to the sky, which is grey and bruised as their hearts. Margaret knew she was dying. She heard the doctor telling her mother that TB was a killer. All Bridget's thoughts are of Margaret. The love she had winging its way to her, making her feel warm, strong and so very sad in one emotional mix.

'I'm going to see Mrs McCann.'

Bridget was out of the house and striding down the path before Tommy realised what she had said. He sat by the fire and worked his way through a pot of tea. Tommy was onto his second pot when Bridget returned and sat in her usual seat by the fire, but everything was far from normal. She stared at the fire for what seemed an eternity,

'Mrs McCann called me an, 'interfering bitch.' She said I was always trying to take Margaret away from her. She must have forgotten how she begged me to look after the bairn.'

Tommy added, 'She's got a convenient memory.'

Bridget carried on re-living the hatred in Mrs Mc-Cann's voice.

'She didn't pull any punches, her language was choice. She never even let me take off me coat. It was as if she was waiting for me. It was frightening. Thirty years is a long time to hold a grudge.'

Tommy spoke quickly and was near to tears.

'She's feeling guilty for what she didn't do. She should have stopped McCann going anywhere near Margaret.'

Tommy and Bridget look hard at each other, knowing, without saying a word, it was Margaret's baby and McCann was the father.

• *No More Groundhog Day* •

IT STARTED ONE FRIDAY IN the bar. I saw Billy, at the end of the night, turn and smile, then slowly put on his overcoat. I didn't say a word. Kept it to myself. I thought that's the way to play it. Say nowt and then you don't get yourself into any bother. I might say something I'll regret. Like when a man and woman have an argument, you side with one or the other and the next thing you know you're cut off their Christmas card list. I could see that in Billy. I had seen him do the same movement week-after-week. When I got home, I thought this is just like my favourite film, 'Groundhog Day.' You know, with Bill Murray and Andie McDowell, when one day is repeated over and over.

The next day, I had just finished watching 'Groundhog' for the third time, and was listening to the usual sounds in the street. The dog was silent. That was unusual. Normally it barks when a fly passes. It's black and barks when anyone trundles by its door. It's not annoying, it's bloody annoying. It was at that precise moment, when the dog wasn't barking, that I picked up my blue pen and I realised I had done this, in exactly the same way, a million times before.

I said out loud, 'No more.'

I had to change. Break the pattern and do something I don't ever do. Change the habits of a life-time. That's when I wrote the notice on my back door, 'No More Groundhog Day.' It was like lancing a boil. The next day my door was covered. And I do mean covered, in notes.

'Every worm has its day and this worm will turn.'

'No more overtime.'

'You pay the television license.'

I don't know if those two knew each other. And there was more.

'I'm sick of working in that bloody shop. I'm serving the same customer again and again.'

The local newspaper wrote an article on me. They had a photograph on their front page, with me standing and smiling at the door. I was pointing at the door handle; someone had drawn what looked like the head of a pig and the words, 'No More,' in Gothic lettering. It must have taken hours. Then it was the turn of the radio and TV to cover the story. And the internet was going wild. I wasn't sure what to tell them. What can you say? I didn't want to mention the bar and Billy putting on his coat. That didn't seem very important and anyway, they were looking, or the TV interviewer said she was 'hunting,' for a big story. It had been a 'dead news day.' That's when I came out with it. I felt, well to be honest, like John Lennon's, 'make love not war.' I heard myself saying things I had never even thought. It all came spilling out.

'No More "Groundhog Day" is the first day of your new life. If you need to leave your partner and get out of a dead marriage. Hand in your notice at work. Today is the most important day of your life. Make the change now.'

I went on for six minutes. I watched the interviewer nod her head, thinking to herself this will be on national television and change my life. Then she motioned to the cameraman to do a close-up on her face as she turned slowly, looking so sincere.

'I feel privileged to be here today at the beginning of a new order, a new religion and way of life, all rolled into one. "No More Groundhog Day Society," is born and I have helped to deliver that child.'

Then she talked about great thinkers, who had influenced the world.

'Karl Marx, Plato, Ruskin and now will the name of James Hall be added to that illustrious list?'

How could I live up to that? That's why I am in hiding. The newspaper, a tabloid, has paid me a small fortune for my story and they have 'exclusive rights.' Whatever that means. I am in Northumberland. Well Blyth, actually, in two rooms above a pub. The newspaper people are next door, playing cards. They said they would put me up in a luxury hotel: 'Luxury?' Paper thin walls and leaky toilet. I've never been out of this room. They've got me wearing this long blonde wig and kaftan thing. You would not believe what people say to you. They have taken to calling me 'The Messiah.' I was shocked at first but you get used to it. Bound to, I suppose.

The cameraman, sent to record my every single movement for the feature they are doing, is always trying to be funny. He asked what did I think about the world economy and what would win the 2.30 horse race at Chepstow? I said put a tenner on 'The Messiah.' It won at ten to one. He's been following me around, bowing and scraping ever since. The trouble is I've had the same thing happen over and over. I know exactly how Bill Murray felt. I half expect Andie McDowell to come in and say, 'Have you seen Phil Connors?'

I don't know if it's this room but something has happened to me. The cameraman keeps coming in and asking about the world economy and what do I fancy in the 2.30 at Chepstow? I have given him the same answer four times over the past six hours. I didn't believe it at first. That's why I've recorded it. He's either a very good actor or I am able to have time repeat and repeat itself. I don't know what to make of it.

I wonder what my mother would think of this. She died eight years ago. I lived with her all me life. Never knew my dad. He died before I was born. Didn't even know his name. He would be surprised to have a Messiah for a son.

Sitting here has given me time to think about life. Their reporter says, 'Contemplation is good for the soul.'

He is very spiritual but does seem to drink a lot of whiskey.

'It goes with the territory,' He says.

I just listen when he talks. I think that's how he believes Messiahs should behave. I've had a very quiet life. Never married. No serious relationship. I worked as a clerk at an engineering firm and when they went bust I got a job as a security man. Mostly nights. Sitting in draughty cabins, with a calor gas fire. I didn't mind. I enjoy my own company. 'Contemplation' isn't a problem.

What I do know is that I don't want to end up like Ned Peterson, the nerd in 'Groundhog Day.' I want to be Phil Connors and have my life changed and learn from it. That's the message of hope in the film. That's not me talking but Halliwell's Film Guide. Not only have I seen the film at least twice a day in the years since it was released but I have read almost everything about it. I was going to go to Punxsutawney (it's in Pennsylvania) but I got myself a computer instead so I can get more information and email the Bill Murray Fan Club.

Having all this information hasn't helped. I still don't know what to do. I would like to think, in some way, I am striking a blow for the little man, the one in the corner of the bar no-one knows much about; that keeps himself to himself, isn't loved too much or hated either but does his bit for society, even if it's just sitting in draughty cabins getting their legs burnt from calor gas fires. I feel as if I should help society. Give people a little hope. I don't know how it's happened but I know this week's winning lottery numbers. Is that what we want from our leaders, our so-called Messiahs? Financial gain?

There is something wrong with the electricity in this place, the lights keep cutting out. Should I give you the winning lottery numbers? Do you have a pen? Your lives will be changed forever. Is that what a Messiah should do? If you haven't a piece of paper, write them on the back of your hand. All the lights have gone. Remember 'No More Groundhog Day.' The numbers are...

DANNY CUDDLES A PLASTIC BAG to his chest, dancing to a frantic beat in his head. The glue, nestling in the bag, feeds him. It is his talk and mutter: his everything. There is someone with him, a new companion on the journey, this odyssey of half-dreams.

The young lads shout at him and there is envy in their cries. They want to be like him: famous. To have their names in the newspaper for causing a disturbance of anyone's peace. He is a star. A major mover in this gluey constellation: the Pied Piper of cheap dreams which block out cold as disappointment bites, rubs him, clings to his clothes. At the bottom of the glue someone tells him,

'You are nothing.'

He injects and breathes and drinks and sucks but at the heart of everything it is still there. He shouts at the false cut-up sky. The words spill into profanities yet they are articulate in his head. His apostles, all friends in glue, billow their plastic bags, holy robes, great magic bagpipes filling their dreams. They look at one another and communicate in gluey Esperanto. This is the moment they speak in tongues and all the nations of glue understand. Grey tongues seesaw down, wisps of clouds from the fiery orb falling from heaven, flowing into their hearts and minds and understanding each other as never before. All these brothers dance to a new beat. Christ and the Apostles had tongues of fire. Danny's acolytes have truth through glue and their eyes shine despite all the hurt they put themselves through. They scream at the sky and the sun bleeds for them.

Danny stumbles and falls and Simon of Cyrene, nor anyone, is there to help. They are some place, somewhere, carrying the cross for anyone but him. Danny shouts, 'Help me for Christ's sake.'

And they point at him and hang him out to dry and two others' spit at him.

He says, 'I'll feed you with my eyes which have the power to make fishes and loaves last forever, blind men see, the dumb speak and lame walk.'

They ignore him.

He is in the park. Propped against a toilet wall with mist smoking through the trees as a woman levitates toward him. She offers him everything. He speaks but when he opens his mouth glue bubbles are a road block to understanding. She washes his face and feet and dries him with her hair which willows across his face. She cries and loves him and he embraces her in this dream as she spreads out his body, like a map she explores. Cold inches in and she disappears and it is then he sees Christ on the cross, and Mary is standing there and she has been true to him, despite everything. Danny's woman has gone; he searches the park, fearing for her, hoping she has not been hurt by people vandals. He prays and feels the black pain of loss. At the cross he sees

Mary Magdalen still standing alone and weeping as tears drape her face and stick like glue only can.

And now loving strangers come and place thorns on Danny's head, made of plastic as they do not want to hurt him. They hold a lance to his side and it drips red as if it were blood. And everything disappears and the end is in sight for this Christ of Glue. His face is frozen as he now slumps against the school wall. A man shouts, a woman screams and children hide as Danny smiles, forgives them and tells them their dreams are now happening, and that they will be realized and love this moment. The words are so wrong; he spits out filth and keeps on shrieking. He cries because he cannot stop the profanities and says, 'Sorry.' His 'sorry' is vile. And the man strikes him and the woman approves and the children are given a warning. And the man turns away, self-righteous as his pulpit face.

Danny cries for everyone. A man picks him up. He is kind and carries him to his chariot with pulsing blue light and sound that bells the universe. Danny lies and smiles and someone says, 'Christ,' they say, 'Christ.'

His life, somehow, is placed in reverse. He is a child at home playing as someone approaches, lifts his clothes, and feels him all over. They are touching him, making him cold and sick and he looks into the man's eyes and it is no stranger. And the man violates Danny who shouts and his mother is deaf as music plays on and on and drowns his sobs.

The ambulance burns through traffic and the blue light trembles on Danny's face and the man wonders what he can do to make things better and says,

'How can I help you my son?'

The man cries, tears dragging down his cheeks, like a broken wheel. Soon Danny will die. He will fight in the ambulance, propel himself around the bed and fight imaginary enemies, bow to crowds and other miracles he has no time to see come to fruition. He will die and he is only thirty-three. They do not cover him and he looks happy as he drops his plastic bag, his thorns of pain. For the first time in a long time, he smiles and offers up his life to all of us.

'Thirty three is no age,' says the man as the ambulance hurries to no avail. Danny's family cry for all his pain and the cross is empty tonight and Christ is no longer on the glue. No longer filling his heart and head with dreams. He is happy for the first time in a long sad time. He dreams and is in the garden and asks his friends, apostles of sorts, to stay with him but they have had too much of something and their eyes are shutters, quickly closing. In this dream he wants to find a higher power, key into a life, other than this. Christ is in the garden. Danny in the ambulance. Christ and Danny are growing close, as if they were images that can be pulled together, to make one. A magic trick: Danny, the gluey and Christ. Danny dreams on and he is standing at the window of a derelict house. It is two in the morning as his companions grumble and cry in their sleep.

Christ kneels, prays and his knees sting with pain as he sweats and wants the strength to embrace death in order that man will live, they will see his death as their redemption. He feels Danny's pain who strives to understand the reasons he cannot articulate, nor obliterate with glue and alcohol chasing cheap dreams in battered rooms. Christ's gown is a peacock purple and glows and Danny sees him as he stands at the window in the derelict house, stretching out his arms and Christ and Danny are growing closer. Christ smiles the most beatific smile. Danny reciprocates and returns to the ambulance with the blue flashing light charging through the crowded council estate, where they know him, heading to the hospital, to be pronounced, 'Dead on Arrival.'

Christ walks in the desert as stars glory above his head and dip themselves into his eyes. He prays, growing nearer to a holy communion with his Father. He feels liberated. So free. Christ sees Danny who stretches out his hands and places his fingers on Christ's brow and knows his hurt. In this final dream Danny sucks his plastic bag and most of the time it is just habit but tonight it is the ultimate high as he mutters, 'It's everything. It is everything.'

He sees himself alone in the park, the others' have gone. This is his desert: graffiti in the shelter, jagged glass and angry dogs snapping at his feet. In the trees birds are silent as the grave he is soon to embrace. He is stripped in the mortuary. A fresh tattoo bleeds on his brow. The coolness of the room dries the gobbets of blood which are dabbed gently by the orderly who does not know why he takes a white sheet and presses it on Danny's face. 'The Mask of Turin' is perhaps what he has in mind. The figure, stamped into the sheet, is of a thirty-three year old glue sniffer and the orderly takes the shroud and places it on top of his meager possessions. There is a crucifix in the room. Christ is on the cross and his side's bleeding and blood limps from his brow and when you look carefully Christ is crying: Danny and Christ are now one.

He pushes him into the container as if it were a great stone that may roll open and he might be seen walking the streets with a tattoo on his brow reading, 'Danny and Christ.'

LOOK AT THIS SCRIBBLED NOTE, 'See you at
seven. Can't wait darling!!!'

Three exclamation marks. They are very popular in this hotel. If they could see they would think the world was full of banging headboards and people shouting, 'Yes. Yes. Yes.' I've seen the lot here: rich, poor, con-men, long-term visitors, one night stands. Lasses on the game, you've got to admire them, it must help to have poor eyesight when you see some of their clients. They always give me a few quid after I say, 'I would hate the management to find out what you're up to.'

The hotel never misses the bits and pieces I take. I need a few extras: mattresses, wardrobes, dressing tables. Not every week, just now and then. I've six wooden huts and a house full of stuff from here. You never know when you might need something. Me husband used to say,

'Doris, what have you got in the cabins?'

I would tell him to go and look but there's no wheelchair access into the back garden. I made sure of that. If you ever want a couple of hundred toilet brushes I am your woman. I cater for all tastes from the fanatically clean and tidy to the 'mildly erotic.' That's what's written on the boxes.

All sorts have been left in these rooms I found methods of torture, after a Salvation Army Conference: black masks and metal studded thongs. How the hell do they walk in them? You name it and I've got it. It'll come in handy one of these days. When I am cleaning a room, I start in the corners; it's always pound coins and Durex packets. No wonder we go through so many beds. This hotel has seen some hanky panky. They've got CCTV in the hallways but none in the rooms. It could be seen as an 'intrusion of privacy' for our guests, that's what the manager's memo said. And it might stop me getting what I want.

My wooden huts, in the back garden, are a maze with a roadblock to stop my husband's wheelchair getting anywhere near. I call him 'Columbo,' you know that detective that's always asking questions. I've told him he's got nowt else to think about. He's always been the same, even when he was working. His accident was a Godsend. It stopped him mooching about the house and garden. I wish he had lost the use of his tongue and legs but that would have been too much to ask. What a moaner, 'I'm stuck in here night and day. The next time I get out will be in a box.'

He might be right. We have separate beds. He sleeps downstairs. I can hear him lying there thinking. He is a very loud thinker. I wish he would disappear. One morning, for me, to come downstairs and all is there is an empty wheelchair.

I cleared one room and got a king size bed out of the hotel. I was on nights, cleaning the restaurant, kitchens and toilets. I knew the security man who has an invalid wife.

'Can't walk a step.' So he said.

I told him my husband was dead to me. He had a bunk bed in one of the walk-in wardrobes in the Security Room. We kept each other company and he showed me how the CCTV worked. You can look closely at some areas and close down others. It's been handy knowing that. The bed was still in its wrapping. I saw the invoice. Cost a bomb. I pushed the dustbins under the bedroom window, dropped the bed down and booked a taxi. The taxi driver gave me a hand. Apparently his wife's an invalid as well. When I got home I used my trolley and put it into cabin seven, it just fitted. You can do anything if you put your mind to it. The security man was moved on. I told the manager he was stealing anything that wasn't nailed down. His wife walked into the office, bold as brass, and collected his belongs. They should have called her Lazarus. They say there was so much stolen stuff in his house it was like Santa's grotto.

Christmas has always been great for me. The stuff that comes through these doors is nobody's business: turkeys, champagne and flowers from some garage. Well, they would just go to waste. I find them a good home. Last Christmas was the best. I worked over the holidays. You get paid extra and Social Services looked after my husband. I told them we are practically divorced and he always cries in front of the woman that comes round on her bike, she has a moustache like that film star Omar Sharif. She made me out to be a monster. She looked after him, took him to a community centre for his Christmas dinner. He didn't want to come home. So 'Omar' took him.

He could have stayed there for me but 'Omar's' mother has dementia and she thought he was her dead husband. They ended-up crying all night and he had to be brought home. He told me the story when I came back at the end of January. I wanted to check on the cabins and make sure there had been no pilfering. I mean, who can you trust? He had lost some weight. 'Omar' had been transferred to another area and through some 'administrative error' she had not been replaced. I went wild on the phone. Somebody came round that night so I could get myself back to work. What do you pay your taxes for?

Anyway, last Christmas there were turkeys, brace-lets, watches, drugs. The lot. The taxi driver and me, the one with the invalid wife, carried out thirty seven cardboard boxes. We dropped them off at a house I am buying and the rest went into my cabins. We did most of it at four in the morning, the dead hours, it's the best time. No nosy buggers wanting to know what you're up to.

They have given me a room at the hotel. I cover for staff that ring in sick. I was 'Employee of the Month' two months on the trot. I told them my husband was in care. I could not look after him any-more what with him being badly incontinent and his bowels evacuating the way they do. People always pull their faces when you talk like that. You have just got to say 'soiled sheets' and they do not want to hear any more. I tell them a story about how I had to pay for a taxi to be fumigated when I was taking him to see his dying brother. I can cry genuine tears when I tell that story. There are times when I think it really happened.

This taxi driver thinks he is my partner, 'partners in crime,' he keeps saying. I don't mind a bit hanky panky. In fact I like a lot of it but he is not my partner. I am going to get rid of him. I know his home number. Apparently his wife's 'pathologically jealous.' That's what he said. They had counselling. I couldn't be bothered with that myself. She already thinks he is seeing the Hotel Receptionist but she wouldn't touch him with a shitty stick. One call and he'll be like that bloke in America, John Wayne Bobbitt, who ended-up dickless. I did the receptionist's voice, on their answerphone, in a dead sexy way, 'I'll see you later Big Boy. Why did you marry that ugly woman when you could have me?'

She dragged him across the hotel foyer. I ran to my room to have a bloody good laugh.

I like the room. Everything I want is here: shower, toilet, comfortable bed and nobody to bother me. Sometimes I go for weeks without talking to anybody. I can think about what I want to do. The thing about a hotel is that nobody's permanent. Everybody's moving on. The managers are only here until they get a bigger or better place, they stay a few months and then they are gone and I'm still here picking up the leftovers.

I've bought another house. Paid cash. Three bedrooms. Full of stuff. I have met a lorry driver. I pay him fifty quid and he drops off whatever I want. I have told him its stuff the hotel wants rid of. He doesn't mind. His wife's another invalid, it's like an epidemic. The hotel reckons on losing fifteen to twenty percent in breakages. I make sure nothing goes missing apart from what I take.

I had to go and see my husband last night. A grown man crying like that. And did he smell. I called the Social Services Emergency Line. They came and sorted him out. I told them I was his sister from Australia and how I was shocked at the state of him and that his wife had always been a cow. They've taken him into Care. He hung onto the carers and pointed at me and screamed, 'Don't let her near me.'

They just nodded their heads and I told them his mother went the same way. I'm going to strip the house and use it for more storage. I usually keep everything but I've burnt all his clothes and our photographs. I've got no use for them. He hung onto this fat lass, with a tight skirt and slip half way down her legs.

He was crying, 'Will you care for me?'

He needs to find out in this life you have to take care of yourself. Once you start relying on others you have had it. That's what my family taught me. My mother and father had it off to a fine art. I made my own meals and went to school by myself from day one. It hasn't done me any harm. My husband always wanted something from me. In the end I could not look at him. I've always been more interested in money. You know how you stand with it. It never lets you down. Pay people to do a job. And that's it. Life is simple.

That's what I do with the lorry driver I've got helping me. He isn't too bright. He believes everything I say. I told him I'm working for a charity and I don't want any publicity. He says I am all heart and keeps saying, 'I'm a lovely woman.' He has started to call me 'Mother Teresa.' In a way I am. I take from the rich and give to the poor, that's me. I mightn't be on the streets of Calcutta but I'm trying to bring more things into my life, 'Mother Teresa of Jarrow,' you know, it's got a ring to it.

I AM GOING TO WRITE THIS DOWN *before I forget. I will add to it as I, sorry, 'we,' go along. I'll not show anyone. It's just something for us. I will give it to Peter when we are together, properly. I mean all the time.*

It's wonderful to be loved, 'really loved.' My boyfriend says, 'I love you,' every day.

Not that I see him that often. He texts me at work. On the bus. He takes selfies and sends them to me, as if I could forget him. I've never been so cared for.

"It's a 'twenty-four seven thing," he says.

Peter setup web pages. One for me and one for him and another for both of us. He added photographs and a video with us in the garden, watching TV, that kind of thing. People started sending me messages. They said how attractive I looked and that they would like to meet me. Peter decided we should just have one site, with him and me.

This texting means we are inseparable. Mam said, it's like some sort of disease. Then walked away. It's unusual for mam to say anything negative.

When I first got a mobile phone I hated it. I saw it as an invasion of privacy. Now they are just part of our lives. Mam says,

'I don't know how you'd manage without that phone; it's always stuck to your ear. You would think he doesn't trust you. He's always checking up on you.'

Mam and dad don't have mobiles. In fact, they were the last people in their street to get a 'proper' phone. You know, a land-line. When they eventually got it, Dad said, 'We'll use it for emergencies.'

They keep it in the cupboard under the stairs. Honest. They bring it out when it rings or when they want to call me on a Sunday, after they have been to church.

I have not written in this diary for ages. I have just found Peter has three mobile phones. He doesn't know that I know. And he doesn't use his proper surname on Facebook.

He is a self-employed joiner. If I asked him he'd say he has the phones to do with his work, his 'contacts.' Now the only people I have contact with are mam and dad. They are retired, their house is paid for and there's only me and my brother. He is married and living in Australia. Dad said he'll pay for me to go to Australia and Peter can look after himself.

I should have added dates to this diary. Too late, now, I suppose.

Me and Peter met when he did a job at my flat. He liked everything about my place, well it's 'ours' now. He said. I've got to start talking like that way, not that he is sharing the mortgage and the house is still in my name. His business is doing well but there's a lot of outlay and he employs men on a part-time basis and they never seem to work out. They're not as good as Peter wants them to be. He can be very demanding.

Peter says, 'You have to work hard at everything, your job and relationships.'

I see mam and dad's marriage and it is a real relationship: a proper partnership. Share and share alike. Dad worked in the Civil Service and mam had lots of part-time jobs when me and my brother were children. Boring they might be as Peter keeps telling me but they are true to one another and honest. I've been doing a lot of thinking about honesty since I found the mobiles.

I have thought about how much time we actually spend together. Take away text messages, telephone calls, not a lot really. I know he comes here, when I am at work. Things have been moved. Photos placed in drawers. And the duvet is on in a different way. I've never said anything.

Today I can hardly write his name since I found Peter's mobiles. I've kept it inside me like a blister in my heart.

'I'm too trusting,' Dad says.

Peter says that's another one of my faults.

Peter will wonder where I am. He gets very concerned. My mobile is ringing. I will let his call go to answer phone. That's the first time I've done that. I feel uncertain.

Dad says, 'Christine, you've got to be strong.'

Mam suffers from agoraphobia. It became worse when I started seeing Peter.

Peter will ring our house phone. I've had it disconnected.

There was only one name on this phone, 'Debbie.' There are hundreds of texts from her and he hasn't deleted any of them. I know why. He loves to feel someone is thinking about him all the time. I eventually had the courage to ring her. She seemed very nice. I said I was doing market research and we just seemed to hit it off.

I said, 'Do you have a boyfriend?'

She told me all about her boyfriend, Peter, a self-employed joiner. Apparently he is always texting and loves her a great deal. She only sees him on Saturdays because he works away all week. She asked about me. I said I was single and ended the conversation. I did leave my number. I just wanted to hear her voice and have an idea of what she was like. I should have just texted.

When you are texting there's not a lot of real conversation is there? What is actually being said? Your imagination adds so much. I mean 'MISS U' is hardly Shakespeare. When I think about what Peter and I talked about there was nothing of any real importance. If you took away his texting finger he would be dumb. 'Abbreviated Platitudes,' was the title of an article I read on text conversations in the dentists. It made perfect sense to me: I LUVED IT.

On the second phone, I texted, as if I was Peter. I told her, 'Caroline,' I wanted her measurements and that she was in for a big surprise. She was a generous sixteen.

I don't really know why I did that. I probably wanted a picture of her so I could dislike her. I felt bad and then I sent over fifty photos of Peter and me and I directed her to our web page. I asked if it was her house and why wasn't he sharing the mortgage? I left my telephone number, on my second mobile phone. I bought it after I found Peter's three mobiles.

Caroline was heart-broken. Peter told her he worked constant nights and that's why he could only see her during the day on a Sunday. I said that's when he was supposed to be seeing his critically ill mother. He told her he was an orphan and had been in Barnardo's. According to him, he was in the same home as the designer Bruce Oldfield. He got Christmas cards from him. He said.

Debbie rang me back. That was the first mobile I rang. She was very aggressive. She wanted to know why I had left my number. She thought I was some sort of hacker. I asked her if she owned her home. She said she did. I said did Peter want her to share? She said they had been to a solicitor and they were about to sign the contracts. I told her everything and said not to contact him for twenty-four hours.

She eventually said, 'Thank you very much.'

Then swore and swore and cried until the battery must have run out.

Phones are an invasion of privacy. I have decided to live without them. I've made a lot of decisions. Mam and dad have helped. And mam has been out of the house for the first time in ages. She walked to my car and I hugged her and she cried.

When she said, 'I'm doing this for you, Christine.'

It was my turn to cry.

I did not want to ring the third phone. I had just come home from crying with mam but I knew I had to contact her. I texted the number as if I was Peter. A text came back straight away, 'Where R U Peter? Me and kids R missing U. We really love U.'

That was me finished. I sat down and sobbed and texted saying, 'Been really busy. Missed U and kids.'

I sent a copy to Peter and the other two girls.

There's nothing like being really loved. My brother, in Australia, rang and said he wants me over there. Then he said, 'We love you and will you please drag mam and dad with you.'

Mam booked the tickets and went to the travel agent by herself. Then we all cried. Dad saw an estate agent and our houses are going to be rented, just to see how Australia goes.

This is the last thing I am going to write in the diary. That'll be the taxi. Mam's crying and smiling at the same time. Dad looks so happy. I know what Peter would have said, 'There is nothing like being loved twenty-four seven.'

• *Elsie Rides Again* •

M Y TWO DEAR FRIENDS, Joan and Billy, let me stay with them after the unpleasant business at the residential home. I told the police it was a fish bone that caught in his throat and that's how he choked. They said I had stood on his oxygen line. 'An unfortunate accident with a fish pie,' is what I told the court. They said there was no sign of fish or fish bone.

They electronically tagged me: eighty-seven years of age and I am being treated like a criminal. They gave me a two-year suspended sentence. The newspaper reported the judge's closing speech; saying I was, 'a menace to society,' what they didn't say was that the judge was drawn to me. He winked when I left the court.

Billy and Joan are the mother and father of my Probation Officer. He felt I would be company for his mam and dad. There has been a little conflict between them as Billy is obviously attracted to me. One night I had a problem with my electric blanket and Billy 'insisted' on helping me. I do not know how we managed to get the duvet over us. My skirt ended-up round my waist and he ran out of the room all hot and bothered then tripped over his trousers. He avoided my eyes for a while but I could tell how he felt. He gets terribly embarrassed. I told him, even at his age, he's seventy-nine; he's bound to get urges around attractive women like myself. What a fuss Joan made. Said I was leading Billy astray and that he was tossing and turning all night. Well, with separate beds, no wonder he gets the way he does. The health visitor, a young woman in her sixties, has to be quick or Billy will have her over Joan's orthopedic chair as quick as you can say, 'pension book.' He gets that look in his eye and you should see the way he leaps onto his motorised scooter. 'Evil Knievel,' I call him. I think he likes it when I say that because he drives away like a lunatic. There would be no separate beds if I were married to Billy. Joan's let herself go. I said to Billy, 'Surgical bandages and the smell of 'Fiery Jack' will do nothing for your relationship.'

Especially as Billy has an acute sense of smell. I notice when I creep up behind him and gets a whiff of my perfume he's away like a bullet; on his scooter to his indoor bowls. Joan was no catch. Billy, on the other hand, was a fine looking man. I've seen their wedding photograph and he seems to be twitching his nose, I don't know if Joan used 'Fiery Jack' then.

I've told Billy he could have done better than Joan. He defended her, of course. I could see the way he was drooling over me that he was looking for a second wife. Joan wasn't long for this world. All it took was something to be left on the top of the stair head. Her built up shoe meant she was very unsteady on her feet.

I arranged the entire funeral. Billy was distraught

and their children were completely useless. They said, "Mother would have wanted to be buried, with a service at 'Saint Joseph's."

I did what I had to do and completely ignored them. I said, "It's going to be, 'Abide with Me' and sixteen minutes in and out of the Crematorium."

I pushed the single beds together. Billy needs comforting. With the electronic tag I couldn't get very far so I put it on Billy. It was just a little bit tight and he screamed like a pig. I shouted at him, 'Shut up, shut up.' His leg bled for two days.

I had a lovely wedding. Billy's family paid for everything: the reception, taxis, flowers, my outfit and I insisted they give me money, it was the least they could do. I bought a king-size bed and a new negligee. Billy is looking more and more gaunt. I don't let him speak. He would just moan about the tag on his leg and why did he always have to be gagged? And why does he just get tomato soup?

He is not the man I thought he was. He is a disappointment and getting more and more unsteady on his feet. I thought Billy wouldn't last much longer. Married three months to the day. I gave him a marvellous send-off. He was my first husband and now I am a respectable widow. I am eligible. Some would say, 'very eligible.'

Billy and Joan's family tried to drive me from the house. I have stood my ground and showed them the will. I got the best solicitor Billy's money could buy. They eventually backed off and said they had suffered enough with the death of their parents.

'Good riddance,' I shouted through the letterbox as they cried their way up the path. I threw Billy and Joan's wedding album in the skip, along with the rest of their family photos. I saw the eldest, the Probation Officer, scrambling in there. I closed the blinds. I have heard nothing from them since.

Now I am friendly with the couple next door. She is ill. Poor soul. I am in here giving her husband a little comfort. He appreciates it. I am sure he does. That's why I'm in their house. She is bed-ridden. Her husband is a lot younger with a full head of hair. He is very sprightly despite walking with those two sticks. They have a home help but he cares for his wife twenty-four hours a day. He is a wonderful man. I asked him to come in for a cup of tea the other night. Just for a break. I could tell he didn't want to leave me. Who could blame him?

I said, 'I'll look after her tonight. Get yourself to the Freemasons.'

I'll give her tomato soup. That will make her sleep. She's barely breathing. She's all skin and bone. This house is immaculate. It is all paid for and they have a lovely little place in Spain. He was a Civil Servant and has a marvelous pension. I had a good look through their paperwork as soon as he went to the Freemasons.

You can see she has been an attractive woman in her time. The eyes are a little bit beady but there's something about her: she looks like me.

'Come on my dear, drink the tomato soup. This will do you the world of good. You'll sleep like a log.'

I can see she's slipping away. God rest her soul. She'll get a good send-off. We will get married in Benidorm. I am pleased I renewed my passport. I've always fancied living in Spain.

• *Tommy, the City and Me* •

WALKING OUT OF THE FLICKERING shadows of the High Level Bridge, I head to the 'Bridge' bar and tappy-lappy down the cobbles to the Quayside and face the new pubs and clubs with taxis devouring customers at the beginning of the month. Ships are missing; the smell of the past has gone. Its Newcastle now and the Millennium Bridge, a barred half-moon, drapes the river. Looking back at the Tyne Bridge, a bunch of Geordie lasses scream at the sky. I see him, near the Guildhall, a bag of rags; blind, empty-eyed and so foul-mouthed it's painful, 'Tommy on the Bridge,' hitting the present. He scrounges tabs from the young lasses before they throw him out of the 'Crown Posada,' the smell of dry piss too much for the early doors, two pint drinkers.

Stag night lads knock Tommy's hat and it slops on the ground as he throws his stick at them and they caw at each other, cling together, throwing coins he gathers in his buckled hands. I leave him turning over the money, trying to make sense of it. Outside the Baltic sun glazes the metal tables and Tommy makes me a shadow, standing in front of me, smelling of shit and beer. I ask who he is. He spits at me, knowing only too well my game, 'Ye'll see us for aa bit but we're aalways heor. Don't forget that mister. Put that in ya story.'

He kicks my chair and it rattles as if I am in a cage. In the 1880s Tommy Ferens would stand on the Swing Bridge, straddling the line between Gateshead and Newcastle to avoid being arrested. He was at it again: not in one place or another. The young manager of the Baltic bar asks him to leave; Tommy walks away with all the pride he can muster, farting so loud the entire bar laughs. I followed him to the Millennium Bridge and then looked upstream at those wonderful bridges and felt a heart bursting pride. Sentimentality rose like sap and I began to cry and stood transfixed. I held the moment as I retraced my past: the Down Beat Club, Club A' Go Go, with the Animals; Mayfair and Cavendish. The music was so loud in my head I had to sit in the Literary and Philosophical Society Library and drown in whispers as bass lines began to fade and whining guitars became background music.

I walk into the Mining Institute and the past erupts, blood seeps from books, miner's amputated arms and legs tangle with their widows, round and around the corridors and I have to leave as Stephenson hands me a lamp and shows me the way out. I am bedazzled by light at the bottom of Westgate Road.

I head to Dobson's Central Station, excited and afraid as a child and I just stop myself from getting on the Metro to the end of the line. Tommy is behind me. I smell him before I see him. I am being stalked by a dead blind man. Tommy died in 1907, collapsing in snow at Gateshead.

Here I am: Central Station to my left, dressed in muffled announcements, diving through traffic heading towards Stowell Street, Chinatown and down the back lane, passing the Morden Tower, buried in poetry and the arse end of restaurants. His heavy breathing's behind me as I fly out of the cobbled lane and pass the Irish Centre with Saint James' Park bending to me. I tried to lose him but he is wise to my every move and with the Haymarket Bus Station and Newcastle University before me, his sickly breath is fresh and strong on my neck. I run down Northumberland Street and head to Shield-field and Byker: he is running me out of town. I stand and eye the bedraggled sky on Byker Bridge, my breathing sharp as a razor and know the past has me. Tommy's harsh voice ringing in my head, 'Th' past's not deed. Put that in ya story mister.'

Acknowledgements

These stories appeared in the following productions or have been published in these magazines:

'Joe and the Boys', *iron* magazine, issue 81/82, 1997; 'Danny and Christ', *Chimera*, Number Three, Winter, 2005, The Penniless Press, on-line magazine, 2015; *Behind The Wall*, play, Customs House, 2001, New Theatre Publications, 2005; 'Running Boy', *the recusant*, on-line magazine, 2010, *The Penniless Press*, on-line magazine, 2015, *The Crazy Oik*, Issue 28, Winter 2016; 'No More Groundhog Day', monologue, Five by One, Customs House, 2006, The Crazy Oik, Issue 31, Autumn 2016; 'Mother Teresa of Jarrow', monologue, Five by One, Customs House, 2006; '24/7', *The Crazy Oik*, Issue 35, Autumn 2017; 'Elsie', monologue, Love in NE32, Customs House, 2002 ; 'Elsie Rides Again', monologue, Five By One, Customs House, 2006, 'Talking Tom', Customs House and tour, 2010; 'Tommy, the City and Me', *Drey* 4, 2012, The Penniless Press, on-line magazine, 2015, *The Crazy Oik*, Issue 27, Autumn 2015.

My thanks to the wonderful Customs House, South Shields, for producing so much of my work over the past twenty years and the editors of the magazines that published these stories.

I also would like to thank all of my lovely family and Sheila Wakefield, Founder Editor, Red Squirrel Press, for their continued encouragement and support.

'Tom is a writer with a gift for dialogue...It would be a challenge to find a funnier piece of black comedy.'

—the *Sunderland Echo*, on 'Elsie'

'Bewildered by what's happened to him, this sad little man unfolds his story for us, evoking sympathy and amusement in almost equal measure.'

—the *South Shields Gazette*, on 'No More Groundhog Day'

'Acutely observed study of human life which is as tragic as it is hilarious.'

—the *Newcastle Journal,* on 'Mother Teresa of Jarrow'

'As her story unfolds, the clichéd exterior is slowly broken down so that we see the appalling reality beneath-and the equally appalling fact that we continue to find her story amusing!'

—the *British Theatre Guide*, on 'Elsie Rides Again'